Farmyard Tales Flip Books
Tractor in Trouble

Heather Amery

Illustrated by Stephen Cartwright

Language consultant: Betty Root
Series editor: Jenny Tyler

There is a little yellow duck to find on every page.

This is Apple Tree Farm.

This is Mrs. Boot, the farmer. She has two children, called Poppy and Sam, and a dog called Rusty.

Ted works on the farm.

He helps Mrs. Boot. Ted looks after the tractor and all the farm machines.

Today it is very windy.

The wind is blowing the trees and it is very cold.
Poppy and Sam play in the barn.

"Where are you going, Ted?"

Ted is driving the tractor out of the yard. "I'm just going to see if the sheep are all right," he says.

Ted stops the tractor by the gate.

He goes into the sheep field. He nails down
the roof of the sheep shed to make it safe.

Poppy and Sam hear a terrible crash.

"What's that?" says Sam. "I don't know. Let's go
and look," says Poppy. They run down the field.

"A tree has blown down."

"It's coming down on Ted's tractor," says Poppy.
"Come on. We must help him," says Sam.

"What are you going to do, Ted?"

Poor Ted is very upset. The tree has scratched his new tractor. He can't even get into the cab.

"Ask Farmer Dray to help."

"I think I can see him on the hill," says Ted.
Poppy and Sam run to ask him.

Soon Farmer Dray comes with his horse.

Farmer Dray has a big, gentle carthorse, called Dolly. They have come to help Ted.

"I'll cut up the tree first."

Farmer Dray starts up his chain saw. Then he cuts off the branches which have fallen on the tractor.

Dolly starts to work.

Farmer Dray ties two ropes to Dolly's harness.
Ted ties the other ends to the big branches.

Dolly pulls and pulls.

She works hard until all the branches are off the tractor. "Well done, Dolly," says Farmer Dray.

Ted climbs up into the cab.

"Thank you very much, Farmer Dray and Dolly,"
he says. And they all go back to the farmyard.

The tractor looks a little messy.

Ted finds a brush and paints over all the scratches.
"It will soon be as good as new," he says.

There's a surprise at Apple Tree Farm.

"Here's your kitten," says Mr. Bran. "She's been in my truck all day and now I've brought her home."

Ted drives them home.

"We'll never find my kitten now," says Sam.
"I'm sure she'll turn up," says Poppy.

"It's the wrong truck."

"Oh dear," says Poppy. "It's not Mr. Bran, and that's not Mr. Bran's truck."

"Stop, Ted, there's a truck."

"I'm sure that's Mr. Bran's truck in that farmyard," says Sam. Ted drives in to see.

Ted, Poppy and Sam round up the sheep.

They drive them back into the field. Ted shuts the gate. "Come on, we must hurry," says Sam.

There are lots of sheep on the road.

"The sheep came out of the field. Someone left the gate open," says Ted. "We must get them back."

Ted looks inside the car.

He mops up all the water. Soon he gets the car
to start again. They drive on to look for the truck.

The car stops in the stream.

"Water in the engine," says Ted. "I'll have to push."
"We'll never find the truck now," says Sam.

Ted drives down a steep hill.

"Look out Ted," says Poppy. There's a stream at the bottom. The car splashes into the water.

Ted stops the car at the crossroads.

"Which way did Mr. Bran go?" says Ted. "There's a truck," says Sam. "It's just going around the bend."

"Perhaps she jumped on the truck."

"Take my car and go after the truck, Ted," says
Mrs. Boot. They jump in the car and drive off.

"Where's my kitten?"

"Where's Fluff?" says Sam. They all look everywhere for Fluff. But they can't find her.

They say goodbye to Mr. Bran.

Apple
Tree Farm

Mr. Bran waves as he drives his truck out
of the farmyard. Ted and Poppy wave back.

Ted works on the farm.

He is helping Mr. Bran, the truck driver. Mr. Bran has brought some sacks of food for the cows.

This is Apple Tree Farm.

This is Mrs. Boot, the farmer. She has two children, called Poppy and Sam, and a dog called Rusty.

Farmyard Tales Flip Books

Kitten's Day Out

Heather Amery

Illustrated by Stephen Cartwright

Language consultant: Betty Root
Series editor: Jenny Tyler

There is a little yellow duck to find on every page.